JACOB'
BEST
SISTERS

For the Broadway Belles—TJ
For Mom and Dad, and Rob and Laura—JF

The illustrator thanks the Ontario Agricultural Museum for its wonderful
preservation of our rural architectural heritage. And a special thank-you to Ben.

Groundwood Books / Douglas & McIntyre Ltd.
585 Bloor Street West
Toronto, Ontario M6G 1K5

Distributed in the U.S. by Publishers Group West
4065 Hollis Street
Emeryville, CA 94608

The publisher gratefully acknowledges the assistance of the
Ontario Arts Council and the Canada Council.

Canadian Cataloguing in Publication Data
Jam, Teddy
Jacob's best sisters
"A Groundwood book".
ISBN 0-88899-229-7
I. Fitzgerald, Joanne, 1956-
II. Title.
PS8569.A427J33 1996   jC813'.54   C96-931163-X
PZ7.J35Ja 1996

Designed by Michael Solomon
Printed and bound in Hong Kong by Everbest Printing Co., Ltd.

JACOB'S BEST SISTERS

BY

Teddy Jam

PICTURES BY

Joanne Fitzgerald

A GROUNDWOOD BOOK

Douglas & McIntyre ✳ Toronto / Vancouver / Buffalo

One day when Jacob got home from school he found a big package on the kitchen table. It was wrapped in brown paper. His name was on the top.

On the sides of the package were big arrows pointing toward the ceiling. Beside them were the words: RIGHT SIDE UP.

"Right side up," said Jacob.

The package was heavy. He knocked on it. It made a funny sound.

Jacob put the box down. It wasn't his birthday and it wasn't Christmas.

Jacob went to the refrigerator and got out the milk. Then he took his favorite bowl, a red plastic spoon, and a box of Chocky Chocko GoodGrain Nutflakes. On the back of the box was a little coupon with a skill-testing question: What color was John A. Macdonald's big black hat?

"Black," said Jacob. Anyone who couldn't answer that question didn't deserve to win a prize. The prize was a cabin just like the ones the pioneers used to have.

Jacob poured Chocky Chocko GoodGrain Nutflakes into the bowl. He looked at the package with the sign: RIGHT SIDE UP.

"Hey," he said. "I won!"

The log cabin was better than it had looked on the cereal box.
The log walls were made out of real wood, and when Jacob opened
the door he could hear a tiny little squeak from the hinges.

It was hard to see inside because the door was so small and his face was so big. In the middle of the kitchen was a round wooden table with four wooden chairs. A couple of them had fallen over.

Jacob got out the penknife he'd received for his birthday. With a knife like this a pioneer could probably cut down a small tree, or at least make a whistle or a toothpick.

He stuck the knife through the door and set the chairs upright. Then he saw that one of the logs had a little bump on it. He used his knife to scrape it smooth.

In the corner of the cabin kitchen was a grandfather clock. Jacob pressed his ear against the door. He was almost sure he could hear the clock ticking.

The roof was supposed to be wooden shingles, but in fact it was shiny plastic, all one piece. Jacob lifted it off. Underneath was a loft with four little beds. In each bed, covered by a tiny patchwork quilt, was a little doll. The dolls' eyes were closed.

At bedtime Jacob's father told him a story about when he was a little boy and he thought his dog had the measles. He had to shave him to make sure, and it took a whole can of shaving cream.

"The pioneers didn't have shaving cream," Jacob said. Then his mother came upstairs, and both his parents kissed him good-night.

"Good-night, Jacob," said Jacob's mother.

"Good-night, Jacob," said Jacob's father.

"Good-night, Jacob!!!!" said four squeaky little voices.

Jacob lay in his bed. He did not move. His parents went out of the room and closed the door.

"Good-night," said Jacob again.

"Goodnight, Jacob!!!!" said four squeaky little voices.

Jacob looked at his log cabin. The moonlight was coming in his window. The cabin was like a real little cabin in the middle of the forest.

He took off the roof. There was a light on in the corner, but all the beds were empty.

Then he looked through the kitchen window and saw the dolls.

"Open the door!!!!" they called.

Jacob opened the cabin door.

The dolls came running out.

"We're hungry!!!!" they cried. "We want something to eat!!!!"

"The pioneers never got hungry," Jacob said. But it was too late. Two of the dolls climbed up Jacob and pulled a package of gum from his pajama pocket. The other two found his school knapsack and his uneaten sandwich from lunch. Soon they were covered in peanut butter and jam.

"We're dirty!!!!" they cried. "We want a bath!!!!"

"The pioneers never took baths," Jacob said. But the dolls ran out of Jacob's room and jumped into the bathroom sink. Soon they were splashing away and using toothbrushes to wash each other.

"What are you doing?" called Jacob's mother.

"Nothing," said Jacob. "What are your names?" he asked the dolls.

"Alice," said one doll.

"Sally," said another.

"I'm Susan."

"Call me Eleanor."

"How did you get into the cabin?"

"That's where we live," Alice said. "Do you have any other clothes? Ours are all wet now."

"We're cold!!!" cried Sally, Susan and Eleanor.

Jacob didn't even bother to tell them that the pioneers walked six miles to school through snow over their heads. He just took the biggest, fuzziest towel in the bathroom, wrapped the dolls in it, and carried them back to his room.

In his dresser he found a white sock that he used to wear when he was little. He took out his penknife.

"This is how the pioneers made clothes," he said. He used the knife to cut the toe off the sock. Then he made a hole in each side. He put the sock over Alice's head and put her arms through the holes.

"There," said Jacob. "What a pretty dress."

"It sticks out in the middle," Alice cried. "It doesn't fit around my stomach."

"That's right!!!" squeaked Sally, Susan and Eleanor.

"I'm not finished yet," Jacob said. He got out his craft kit and cut a small strip of leather for a belt. "There," he said. "How's that?"

"It's beautiful," Alice said. "Thank you, Jacob."

She jumped into Jacob's arms and gave him a big hug. Then the other dolls also jumped into Jacob's arms.

"There," said Jacob. "Is everyone happy?"

"No! No! No!" squeaked the three other dolls. "We want to look nice, too. We want new dresses."

"You came to the right place," Jacob said.

He looked in his drawer. He found a pair of red-and-green striped socks that had holes in their toes. "Me first! Me first! Me first!" squeaked the dolls.

"You have to take turns," said Jacob. "The pioneers sometimes had to wait ten years for a dress."

The dolls began to cry.

"Just kidding," Jacob said. "The first one to be quiet gets the next dress."

Sally clapped her hand over her mouth. Susan and Eleanor did the same.

Jacob used his knife to fix up one of the striped socks. Then he took a piece of leather from his craft box and made Sally a tiny apron.

"Thank you," Sally said.

"You're welcome," said Jacob. "You are a very polite doll."
"Now me! Now me!" squeaked the other two dolls.
Jacob picked up the doll with light brown hair.
"You can go next, Susan," he said. He made her a dress just like
Sally's dress, except that around its waist was a belt with long fringes.

"Don't forget me!" Eleanor cried.

"I have an idea," Jacob said. He took out a handkerchief his grandmother had given him and wrapped it around Eleanor. Then he used a little piece of string to tie it on.

"Why am I wearing a tablecloth?" Eleanor sniffled.

"That's a fancy dress," Jacob said. "Now you look like a pioneer princess going to a barn dance."

The other dolls clapped and shouted, "Eleanor is a pioneer princess!!!"

Jacob picked up all the dolls and put them on his bed.

"Now, is everybody happy?"

"Yes!!!!" the dolls cried. "Let's play hide-and-seek." They ran out the door and hid in Jacob's parents' room. Jacob searched all over and finally found them under the bed. When he tried to pick them up, they escaped out the other side and discovered his mother's dressing table and jewelry box.

"What are you doing up there?" called Jacob's mother.

"Nothing," Jacob called back.

The dolls threw down the necklaces and rings and earrings and ran back to Jacob's room. Jacob shut them in, then cleaned up his mother's jewelry.

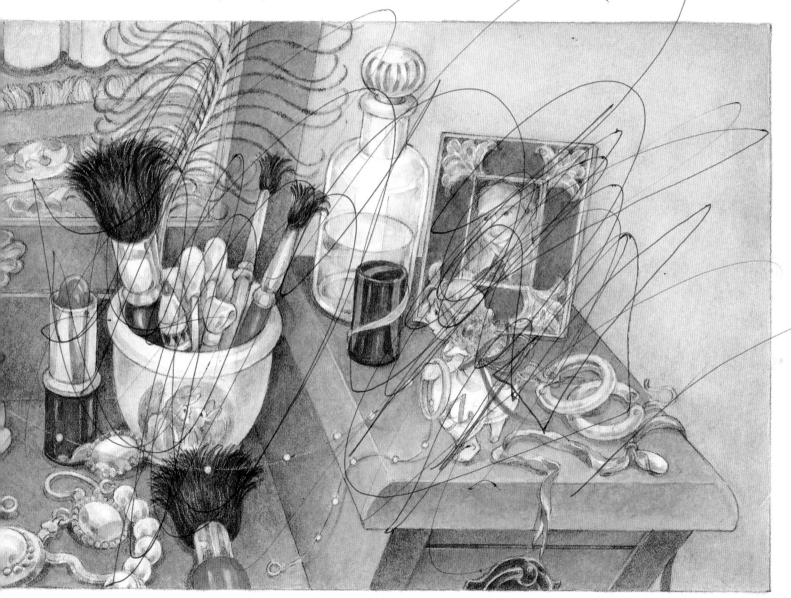

When he got back, Alice was telling Sally and Susan a story.
Eleanor was crying.

"Oh, dear," said Jacob. "Is anything wrong?"

"No," said Eleanor. "It's just that Susan has stripes and I don't."

"That's terrible," Jacob said. He found three gold stars. He stuck
them on her dress.

"Thank you," Eleanor sniffled. "Now I really do look like a
pioneer princess."

Jacob was getting tired. He put the dolls into their beds and tucked their covers under their chins.

Then he turned out the lights and climbed into bed. The moon came in the window and turned the dollhouse back into a real log cabin in the middle of a forest.

He closed his eyes. "Good-night, Alice," he said. "Good-night, Sally. Good-night, Susan. Good-night, Eleanor."

"Good-night, Jacob!!!!"

Just as he was falling asleep, the dolls landed on his chest. "We're lonely!!!!" they cried. "Tell us a story!!!!"

"All right," Jacob said. "Once upon a time there was a little boy who wanted a log cabin. He was a very lonely little boy, and when he got the log cabin he was going to pretend he lived there with a friend and they were pioneers."

"We have a log cabin!!!!" the dolls squealed. "Come live with us!!!!"

"Thank you," Jacob said.
"What are you doing now?" called his mother.
"Telling myself a story," Jacob said.
"Good-night!" his mother called.
"Good-night," Jacob said.
"Good-night!!!!" whispered four little voices.

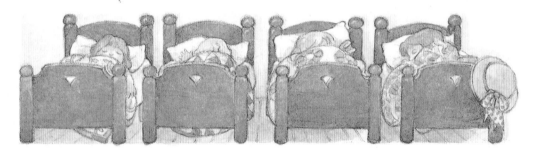

In the morning Jacob looked under the roof of his log cabin. The dolls were still asleep.

He got dressed and went down to breakfast.

"Did you have any dreams?" his father asked.

"I don't know," said Jacob. He opened a new package of Chocky Chocko GoodGrain Nutflakes. It had a picture of a sailing ship with four little sailors standing on the deck.

"This is what I'm getting next," said Jacob.